BERWYN PUBLIC LIBRARY
P9-CQF-804
1063
DISCARD

ENCYCLOPEDIA BROWN

and the Case of the Treasure Hunt

DONALD J. SOBOL

Illustrated by GAIL OWENS

A YEARLING BOOK

For the Townleys—
Susan, George, Bryan,
Laura, and Brent

Published by Yearling, an imprint of Random House Children's Books
a division of Random House, Inc., New York

Visit us on the Web! www.randomhouse.com/kids

Educators and librarians, for a variety of teaching tools, visit us at
www.randomhouse.com/teachers

ISBN: 0-553-15650-0

Reprinted by arrangement with Yearling Books

Printed in the United States of America

August 2002

38 37 36 35 34

Contents

The Case of the Masked Robber

In police stations across the United States, the same question was asked again and again.

Why did every grown-up or child who broke the law in Idaville get caught?

Idaville looked like an ordinary seaside town. It had clean beaches, two delicatessens, and three movie theaters. It had churches, a synagogue, four banks, and a Little League.

What made Idaville different from anyplace in the world was a redbrick house on Rover Avenue. For there lived ten-year-old Encyclopedia Brown, America's Sherlock Holmes in sneakers.

Encyclopedia's father was chief of police. When Chief Brown came up against a crime that he could not solve, he knew what to do. He put on his hat and went home to dinner.

At the table, he told Encyclopedia the facts of the case. Usually Encyclopedia solved the mystery before dessert. If he needed a few extra minutes, his mother was disappointed.

Chief Brown never told anyone the secret of his success. Who would believe him?

Who would believe that the brains behind Idaville's war on crime hadn't yet raised the seat of his two-wheeler?

Encyclopedia never let slip a word about the help he gave his father. He didn't want to seem different from other fifth-graders.

But he was stuck with his nickname. Only his parents and teachers called him by his real name, Leroy. Everyone else called him Encyclopedia.

An encyclopedia is a book or a set of books filled with facts from *A* to *Z*. So was Encyclopedia's head. He had read more books than anyone in Idaville, and he never forgot a word. His pals said he was better than a library for getting answers. He was never closed.

Tuesday evening, Chief Brown took his seat at the dinner table. He looked at his soup without picking up his spoon.

Encyclopedia and his mother knew what that meant. He had a case he could not solve.

"Tim Crandan was robbed in his home early today," Chief Brown said. "The case is a puzzle."

"Tell Leroy about it, dear," Mrs. Brown urged. "He's never failed you."

Chief Brown nodded. He took a small notebook from the breast pocket of his uniform. Using his notes, he went over the case for Encyclopedia.

"Shortly after sunrise," Chief Brown said, "Mr. Crandan was awakened by noises in his living room. He surprised a robber."

"Who is Mr. Crandan?" Mrs. Brown asked.

"For thirty years he taught tennis in Alabama. He retired last year and moved to Idaville," Chief Brown answered.

He looked back at his notes and continued. "Mr. Crandan saw a masked man making off with his three Chinese screens. The masked man pulled a gun and tied Mr. Crandan to a chair. Mr. Crandan watched through a window as the robber loaded the screens into a station wagon and drove off."

"How valuable are the screens?" Mrs. Brown asked.

"Each has six panels of ivory figures," Chief Brown said. "Mr. Crandan has them insured for a huge amount of money."

"Aren't there any clues?" Mrs. Brown inquired.

"A good one," Chief Brown said. "As Mr. Crandan entered the living room, the robber saw him and hurriedly put on a mask. He wasn't quick enough. Mr. Crandan recognized him but was afraid to say anything. The robber might have used his gun if he thought he'd been recognized."

Mrs. Brown glanced at Encyclopedia as if expecting him to speak. The boy detective was not ready to ask his one question. Usually he needed to ask only one question to solve a case at the dinner table.

So Mrs. Brown asked a question herself. "If Mr. Crandan knows who robbed him, why haven't you made an arrest?"

"Because," replied Chief Brown, "the man he recognized is one of the Enright twins, Fred or Carl. They look exactly alike. Mr. Crandan couldn't tell which twin was the robber."

"I don't know the twins," Mrs. Brown said. "What do they do?"

"Fred Enright was a store clerk," Chief Brown replied. "Carl Enright was a top professional tennis player for twenty years. Both men are retired. Fred moved to Idaville six months ago. Carl followed him a month later. Each lives alone."

"What about an alibi?" Mrs. Brown asked. "Where were the twins when Mr. Crandan was robbed?"

Chief Brown flipped a page in his notebook. "Fred claims he didn't get up until eight o'clock today, more than an hour after the robbery. Carl says he slept until nine. Neither has a witness to back up his story."

"So neither has a real alibi," Mrs. Brown stated.

"For that matter, neither does Mr. Crandan," Chief Brown pointed out. "He could be making up a story about a robbery."

"I see—then he can get the insurance money and still keep the Chinese screens," Mrs. Brown murmured. "But why would he say one of the twins robbed him?"

"Mr. Crandan dislikes them," Chief Brown

replied. "They dislike him. I don't know why, but it has something to do with a tennis tournament many years ago."

"Mr. Crandan may have faked the robbery," Mrs. Brown said, "and he's trying to blame one of the twins."

"Mr. Crandan doesn't have a criminal record," Chief Brown pointed out. "But the twins do. They spent a year in jail in Alabama two years ago for stealing oil paintings."

"Then turn everything around," Mrs. Brown said thoughtfully. "The robber didn't put on his mask until Mr. Crandan entered the living room because he *wanted* Mr. Crandan to see his face."

Chief Brown frowned. "The robbery might be a clever trick. The twins could be setting Mr. Crandan up. If he accuses one of them of stealing the screens and can't prove which one, he'll look foolish. Good heavens, what a twist!"

Mrs. Brown glanced at Encyclopedia again. The boy detective had closed his eyes. He always closed his eyes when he did his deepest thinking on a case. Suddenly his eyes opened.

"What was the robber wearing, Dad?" he said.

"Dark trousers and a white, short-sleeved

shirt," Chief Brown answered.

"Leroy," Mrs. Brown said, obviously disappointed by the question. "How can his *clothes* be important?"

"Not all his clothes, Mom," Encyclopedia replied. "Just his shirt. It tells us who is guilty."

WHY?

(*Turn to page 72 for the solution to The Case of the Masked Robber.*)

The Case of the Round Pizza

Throughout the year Encyclopedia helped his father solve mysteries. During the summer he helped the children of the neighborhood as well.

When school let out, he opened his own detective agency in the family garage. Every morning he hung out his sign:

The last customer Monday was Farnsworth Grant. Farnsworth, who was ten, had founded the Idaville Flat Earth Association.

"If the earth were round, people in Australia would be hanging upside down," he insisted.

When he came into the Brown Detective Agency, he wasn't having fun with the earth, round or flat. He was concerned with something round *and* flat.

"Bugs Meany stole my pizza!" he blurted.

Encyclopedia groaned. "Bugs, forever Bugs."

Bugs Meany was the leader of a gang of tough older boys. They called themselves the Tigers. They should have called themselves the Spoons. They were always stirring up trouble.

Farnsworth explained what had happened. His mother was feeling ill, so he had volunteered to bring home a pizza for dinner.

"Ten minutes ago I was carrying the pizza when Bugs stopped me," he said. "Bugs looked into the box and helped himself to a piece. Then he said I was just the kind of kid he needed."

"For what?"

"To join his new society," Farnsworth answered. "It's called the Society to Preserve the Round Pizza. He said he needed concerned citizens like me as members."

"I can guess what happened next," Encyclopedia remarked. "Bugs said you could join his society if you paid the dues. Since you didn't have enough money, he took the rest of the pizza in payment."

"You know Bugs, all right," Farnsworth said bitterly. He laid twenty-five cents on the gas can beside the detective. "I want to hire you. Get back my pizza!"

"It may be too late," Encyclopedia warned. "But we'll talk with Bugs. Come along."

"Not me," Farnsworth said.

"Why not?" Encyclopedia demanded impatiently. "Give me one good reason."

"I'll give you three," Farnsworth replied. "I'm afraid, I'm scared, I'm a coward."

"Relax," Encyclopedia said gently. "I've handled Bugs before. His breath is worse than his bite."

The Tigers' clubhouse was an unused toolshed behind Mr. Sweeney's Auto Body Shop. Bugs and two of his Tigers were outside, sitting on orange crates.

TIGERS

"Well, well," Bugs growled as Encyclopedia and Farnsworth approached. "Look who's playing hooky from a padded cell."

Farnsworth walked straight up to the thin pizza box that lay open on the clubhouse step. One piece of pizza remained.

"They've eaten nearly all of it!" Farnsworth screamed.

"Man, oh, man," Bugs moaned, clapping himself on the forehead. "Do I ever get the screwballs! What's he raving about?"

"Farnsworth claims you stole a slice of his pizza, and then you stole the whole thing," Encyclopedia said.

"This pizza belongs to us Tigers," Bugs retorted. "We bought it to celebrate the one-month anniversary of the Society to Preserve the Round Pizza."

"What's that?" Encyclopedia inquired.

"It's not a useless society, like the Flat Earth Association," Bugs declared with a sneer. "When you talk pizza, you're talking something you can get your teeth into."

"Who cares?" Farnsworth cried.

"All true pizza lovers care," Bugs answered loftily. "Say, what's the matter with you? Haven't you heard? The square pizza was on the edge of cornering the market until we Tigers met the challenge. We started our society to keep the round pizza rolling along."

"Never mind the news brief," Farnsworth said. "You stole my pizza!"

"I told you it belongs to us," Bugs snapped. "Now you two crumb cakes move on. Go kiss a shark. Stick around and we'll play chimes."

"What's . . . ch-chimes?" Farnsworth's voice faded as he watched Bugs curl his fingers into fists.

"First I ring your head, and then I ring your neck," Bugs snarled.

"I have a suggestion," Farnsworth whispered to Encyclopedia. "Let's get out of here before we are severely injured."

Encyclopedia ignored the plea. He knew that if he stood calmly, Bugs would shed his tough-guy act.

Bugs did. "There's no sense in arguing," he said when Encyclopedia refused to scare. "Here, have a piece of pizza. We Tigers share everything equally. We each had a couple of pieces, so you can have the last one."

"Thanks," Encyclopedia said. "Do you have a knife to cut it in half?"

Bugs looked questioningly at the other

Tigers. They shook their heads.

"I'm not settling for half a piece of my own pizza," Farnsworth said.

"You won't have to," Encyclopedia replied. "Bugs will buy you another. His story is too much to swallow."

WHAT WAS BUGS'S MISTAKE?

(Turn to page 74 for the solution to The Case of the Round Pizza.)

The Case of Bugs's Zebra

What Bugs Meany wanted most out of life was to get even with Encyclopedia Brown.

The Tigers' leader hated being outsmarted all the time. He longed to shove the detective's teeth so far down his throat that he'd have to do deep knee-bends to chew.

Still, Bugs never tried bullying Encyclopedia. Whenever he got mad enough to use muscle, he remembered Sally Kimball.

Sally was Encyclopedia's junior partner. She was also the prettiest girl in the fifth grade, and the best athlete. What's more, she had done what no one had thought possible.

She had pounded rough, tough Bugs Meany dizzy.

The last time they had fought, Bugs finished on his back, lost in dreamland. "Your money will be cheerfully refunded, madam," he had moaned.

"Bugs won't quit till he gets even with you," Encyclopedia warned Sally. "You've punched out his lights too often."

"He's not exactly fond of you, either," Sally replied. "Heck, why worry? Bugs thinks he's a tiger, but he's really just an animal cracker."

The detectives were riding the number four bus to the zoo in Glenn City. The previous evening, Sally had received a telephone call from a boy who had given his name as Phil Birch.

He had engaged the detectives by telephone. He asked them to pick up a white shopping bag that he had left at the zoo that day. He couldn't go himself, he said, because he was sick. In the shopping bag were a few marshmallows and a birthday gift, a box of chocolates, for his mother.

As the detectives got off the bus, Sally looked worried. "I don't know a Phil Birch," she said. "I wonder if this is another of Bugs Meany's tricks. We could be walking into a trap."

"We'll just have to watch our step," Encyclopedia murmured.

"Phil Birch said he may have left the shopping bag under a bench near the antelopes," Sally said.

The crowd at the zoo was light, and the detectives reached the antelope enclosure quickly.

Encyclopedia saw the bench right away. It stood among a cluster of small palm trees. Under the bench was a white shopping bag.

Sally peered into the bag. "A few marshmallows and an unopened box of chocolates, just as Phil Birch said," she told Encyclopedia.

Suddenly a voice shouted, "There they are!"

It was Bugs Meany. He carried a sketch pad. As he ran toward Encyclopedia and Sally, he called, "Guard! Guard!"

In a moment a uniformed guard approached, striding hurriedly.

Bugs wagged a finger under Sally's nose. "Thought you could make a fool of the law, eh, sister?" he cried.

MONKEYS
BEARS
LIONS
ANTELOPES

"Sister?" Sally exclaimed. "If that's true, I'm leaving home."

"What's this about?" Encyclopedia demanded.

"They were feeding the antelopes candy," Bugs said. "Oh, how cruel! Everyone knows that too much sugar gives animals heart problems."

"We didn't feed them a thing," Sally protested. "You're trying to frame us."

"I saw you throwing marshmallows at the antelopes," Bugs declared.

The guard held out his hand. "May I see what's in the shopping bag?"

"Marshmallows and chocolates," Sally said in a small voice.

"Cruelty to animals is an offense punishable by law," Bugs sang. "Arrest them!"

"Not so fast," the guard said. "I didn't actually see the young lady feed the animals, and there is no one else around. Are you sure of what you saw, young man? Be honest."

"Honesty is my weakness," Bugs said. "I saw them tossing marshmallows to the antelopes not two minutes ago."

"You living lump," Sally said, raging. "You know you're lying."

"Lying?" Bugs cried. "I don't know the meaning of the word."

"Judging by your grades, you don't know the meaning of lots of words," Sally retorted.

"What are you doing at the zoo today, Bugs?" Encyclopedia asked.

"And so conveniently close to us," Sally added.

"I was drawing a zebra," Bugs answered slyly. He flipped open his sketch pad and showed it to the detectives. "I'd just finished this sketch when I spotted you two tossing marshmallows to the antelopes."

Encyclopedia looked at the zebra enclosure, fifty yards to his left. Then he looked at the drawing, a pencil sketch of a zebra. On one of the white body stripes, running from the front to the hind legs, Bugs had written his name and the date.

"Artists don't sign their names in the center of a picture," Sally said. "They sign at the bottom."

"When you're good, you don't have to be modest," Bugs said, gloating.

"You planned this whole thing, you babbling brook," Sally snapped. "You had one of your Tigers call me and pretend to be Phil

Birch. That's how you got us here."

"A true artist like me never gets mixed up with juvenile delinquents," Bugs declared. He clasped his hands over his heart and inhaled deeply. "Ah, how I long for some quiet place to paint, a place where the hand of man has never set foot."

"You talk worse than you draw, Bugs," Encyclopedia said. "I can prove you're trying to frame us!"

WHAT WAS THE PROOF?

(*Turn to page 76 for the solution to The Case of Bugs's Zebra.*)

The Case of the Treasure Hunt

Every July 9, the town of Idaville celebrated Founders Day. The big event for children was the treasure hunt.

The hunt always began at a glass display case in the main library. The display case housed the diary of Samuel Dowdy. He had helped found Idaville.

Encyclopedia and Sally joined the other children waiting for the hunt to begin. Everyone knew the rules. Nevertheless, Mr. McPherson, the hunt director, went over them thoroughly.

This year, he said, the clues were hidden at

five checkpoints. Each clue told where the next checkpoint was. Hunt officials made sure every boy and girl reached every checkpoint and found the clue there. No one could cheat by simply following the leaders.

A red card was hidden at the fifth and last checkpoint. On it were written two words: "You Won."

"The winner's prize this year is a racing bicycle," Mr. McPherson announced. "Here is your first clue."

He read from a piece of paper. "Go to Clarson. Hurry up and get the lead out of your gas."

"That must mean the next clue is hidden at Dan's Service Station on Clarson Avenue," Sally whispered to Encyclopedia.

The detectives moved quickly toward the front door of the library. Mr. McPherson stopped them.

"I must see you at once," he said in a low, worried tone. He led Encyclopedia and Sally to a corner.

There he explained his concern. An hour ago, as he hid the clues, he sensed someone watching him.

"Whoever it was," he said, "knows the

checkpoints and the clues. He or she is sure to win."

Mr. McPherson looked at Encyclopedia steadily.

"I don't want to go to the police," he continued. "It would spoil the treasure hunt."

Encyclopedia nodded in agreement. "You want us to find the cheater?" he asked.

"And keep it quiet," Mr. McPherson cautioned. "I understand you are good at such matters. Will you help?"

"I'll do my best," Encyclopedia replied, though it meant withdrawing from the treasure hunt. "What is the final clue? The one that leads to the card with 'You Won' written on it?"

" 'Look beneath the best-known dairy in town,' " Mr. McPherson replied.

"That's too easy," Sally complained. "There is only one dairy in town, the office building of the Johnson Dairy Company."

"Yes, but what most people don't know is that there is a little four-car garage below the building," Mr. McPherson said. "You enter it from a side alley. The card 'You Won' is tucked behind the windshield wiper of a pickup truck."

NO LOUD TALKI
PLEASE

Encyclopedia closed his eyes in thought. When he opened them, he said, "All we have to do is move the card from the underground garage to a new place."

"But that will mean changing the wording of the last clue," protested Mr. McPherson.

"Exactly," Encyclopedia said. "But it's important that the cheater doesn't notice the change. If he does, he'll be frightened off. We'll never know who he is."

"Or who *she* is," Sally said tartly.

Encyclopedia accepted the correction with a smile. To Mr. McPherson he said, "You only have to switch two letters in the clue that leads to the Johnson Dairy Company and the 'You Won' card."

Encyclopedia whispered the two letters into Mr. McPherson's ear and told him where to hide the "You Won" card.

"By George, young man," Mr. McPherson exclaimed. "That is brilliant!"

Mr. McPherson shook hands with the detectives and went off to set the trap. He had to rewrite the last clue and put a new "You Won" card where Encyclopedia had advised him.

"Will you please tell me what's going on?"

Sally protested. "I want to know how you are going to catch the cheater without anyone finding out."

Encyclopedia explained his plan as they biked to the Johnson Dairy garage.

Sally looked at him with a mixture of awe and anger. "Why didn't I think of that?" she grumbled.

They rode in silence the rest of the way to the garage.

"There it is," Encyclopedia said.

The red "You Won" card was under the windshield wiper of a pickup truck where Mr. McPherson had tucked it. Encyclopedia tore up the card.

"Now we wait," he said.

After what seemed forever, Sally nudged Encyclopedia, and they ducked behind the pickup truck.

Regina Castleberry was coming down the ramp from the alley.

"That figures," Sally said under her breath. "I know Regina. The only time she's in bad company is when she's alone."

"Sssh," Encyclopedia warned. "We don't know anything yet."

Regina walked to the pickup truck. She

stared at the empty windshield wipers, puzzled.

Encyclopedia stood up. "Looking for something?"

Regina was startled, but she recovered herself. "Yeah, the winning card in the treasure hunt."

"What made you think it was here?" Sally demanded.

"The last clue said it was," Regina replied. "Say, why are you two hanging around? You ought to be out playing with squirrels."

"We've been waiting for the cheater who followed Mr. McPherson as he laid out the treasure hunt," Encyclopedia said. "And you're the one."

WHAT MADE ENCYCLOPEDIA SO SURE?

(*Turn to page 78 for the solution to The Case of the Treasure Hunt.*)

The Case of the Stolen Jewels

On Saturday Encyclopedia and Sally closed the Brown Detective Agency early and biked to the ocean.

They planned to swim, read, and relax in the sun. They didn't expect to solve a mystery. Neither did they expect to meet Dustin Durant.

Dustin was eleven and a photography whiz. When Encyclopedia and Sally spotted him, he was taking a picture on the path that overlooked the beach. His subjects were a man, a woman, and the President of the United

States. The woman was shaking hands with the President—kind of.

Dustin pulled the picture from his camera. The man showed the picture to the woman, and they walked away chuckling. The President remained motionless.

Encyclopedia and Sally parked their bikes and hurried over for a closer look.

The "President" was a life-size, black-and-white photograph mounted on plywood.

Encyclopedia admired the propped-up President, who was standing straight as a board and smiling stiffly. His right arm was outstretched, ready for the next cash customer.

"Gosh, Dustin, what a great idea!" Sally exclaimed. "How much do you charge?"

"Five dollars for a black-and-white picture, and three dollars if the customer wants to use his own camera and film," Dustin answered. "But for the two of you, it's on the house."

The detectives posed gleefully. They took the picture proudly to the beach, where for ten minutes they had peace and quiet. Then Dustin came flying across the sand.

"Some man just stole my camera!" he cried. "Dad will have a fit!"

He explained. His father, a professional photographer, had made the cutout of the President. Dustin took the picture and collected the money.

"You've got to recover Dad's camera!" Dustin wailed.

"Calm down and tell us what happened," Sally said.

"After I took your picture, two men sat down right over there," Dustin replied, pointing to a bench near the cutout President. "They were saying some pretty strange things."

"What do you mean?" Encyclopedia asked.

"I couldn't hear everything," Dustin said. "But the tall man said something about 'delivering the goods' this afternoon to the house on Highland Avenue. The short man nodded and said he'd better write down the exact address before he forgot it. Then the tall man said, 'Don't write anything down. Keep it in your head. Just remember—it's the last upside-down year. The next one won't come for more than four thousand years.' "

Sally frowned, puzzled. "What happened then?"

"They got up from the bench and separated," Dustin said. "The short man decided he wanted a snapshot with the President. I'd just clicked his picture when the tall man rushed back and grabbed the camera. 'You crazy fool, having your picture taken!' he yelled at the short man. Then they both took off fast with the camera and the picture."

"Can you describe the two men better?" Encyclopedia asked.

"The short man had red hair and his left arm was in a sling," Dustin said. "The tall man was bald and had a dark mustache."

Encyclopedia whistled. "Those descriptions fit the two men who held up Polk's Jewelry Store yesterday, except they were wearing women's sheer stockings over their heads."

"I'll bet the short man was told to leave the stolen jewels at a house on Highland Avenue," Sally said. "Let's go there and watch for them."

Encyclopedia agreed. After Dustin stored the "President" in the first-aid station, the three children rode the number three bus to Highland Avenue.

As they alighted, Sally's face was a study in

gloom. "I forgot that Highland Avenue is twenty blocks long. We can't watch every house."

Encyclopedia said nothing. He continued walking. After five blocks he remarked quietly, "This is the house—the gray one on the right."

"How do you *know* this is the house?" Sally whispered.

Before Encyclopedia could answer, a blue car drove up and stopped in the driveway. A short man with his left arm in a sling got out. He was carrying a briefcase.

"He's one of them!" Dustin gasped.

"The stolen jewels may be in the briefcase," Encyclopedia murmured. "Time to call the police."

He made the call at the public telephone on Quincy Road. When he returned to the hedge, he saw that the short man had come out of the house.

The man no longer had the briefcase. He stopped and stared at the hedge.

"He's spotted us!" Dustin yelped. *"Run for your life!"*

There was no need to run. A patrol car had pulled in front of the gray house. The short man bolted, but he was quickly captured.

Within two hours, the police work was done.

The gray house belonged to Baldwin Van Carson III, a banker with a sideline in stolen goods. The jewels from the holdup were found in the briefcase in his bedroom closet. The short man, frightened, turned informer; his partner, the tall man, was arrested in a motel on Ocean Drive. Dustin got his father's camera back.

At police headquarters, Chief Brown congratulated Encyclopedia. "How did you figure out which house to watch?" he asked.

"I'd like to know, too, Encyclopedia," Sally said. "In all the excitement, you never told me!"

HOW DID ENCYCLOPEDIA KNOW WHICH HOUSE TO WATCH?

(*Turn to page 80 for the solution to The Case of the Stolen Jewels.*)

The Case of the Painting Contest

Pablo Pizzaro was Idaville's greatest child artist.

The fifth-grader had won first prize at the Talent Day in April. His winning statue, titled *Bumps on a Log,* was carved out of three potatoes.

"It invites the viewer to eat his art out," Pablo had explained to his friends.

Frankly, Encyclopedia thought *Bumps on a Log* was small potatoes. He dared not say so, however, in front of Sally. She became fluttery whenever she was near Pablo.

"If Pablo wins a prize at the Modern Art Festival today, fame will be within his grasp," Sally said dreamily.

Encyclopedia kept a straight face. "True," he agreed. "Art lovers yet unborn will praise his name."

The Modern Art Festival was held in the high-school gym. The detectives saw Pablo as they entered.

The young artist was dressed for the part. He wore a beret, a tan smock, and a huge, floppy bow tie.

"He looks gift-wrapped," Encyclopedia thought.

"What have you in the show, Pablo?" Sally asked.

"Nothing," replied Pablo. "No other kid would enter a painting or a sculpture against me. So the children's division was dropped this year."

"Oh, that's unfair," Sally said.

"I've entered the speed-painting contest," Pablo said. "It's open to any amateur artist in the state. How fast you paint counts more than how well you paint."

He led the detectives to a corner of the gym.

A group of modern art lovers gazed at a white canvas set upon an easel. "What soul—superb!" a woman gushed. "A major breakthrough!"

"The canvas is white because it hasn't been painted on yet," Pablo whispered disgustedly.

A man with a judge's badge moved the onlookers back. "Our first speed-painter," he announced, "is John Helmsly, a sea captain."

"Here and ready!" responded a bearded man. He strode to the canvas. In one hand, he carried a board with blobs of paint. In the other hand, he held a square-tipped knife.

The judge gazed at his stopwatch. "On your mark, get set, go!"

John Helmsly began whacking paint wildly against the canvas with the knife.

"I don't use brushes," he said, panting. "They take too long to clean."

The knife flew . . . *whack, whack, whack.* Soon a boat, water, and sky were visible to onlookers with a helpful imagination.

"The boat is moving at about only four knots an hour," John Helmsly said. "So we need just a touch of foam where the front cuts the water, and a little behind. And here's the

skipper at the back looking at a map of where he's going. There—done! I shall call it *Sailboat in Motion.*"

"Two minutes and fifty-eight seconds," the judge announced.

"H-he broke three minutes!" Pablo said, shocked. "My best time in practice for the same size painting is four minutes and eight seconds."

Encyclopedia was shocked, too. *Sailboat in Motion* might be instant art, but it was the worst picture he had ever seen.

"That's one new painting that won't become an old masterpiece," he said.

"Maybe he just slopped paint on the canvas and named it whatever it looked like," Sally suggested.

"No," Pablo replied. "A contestant must describe what he's painting as he goes along. And he can't be a professional artist. Those are the rules."

"John Helmsly sure didn't lie about himself," Sally declared. "He never said he was an artist."

Encyclopedia had seen enough.

"When is your turn, Pablo?" he asked.

"There are twelve artists entered in the

speed-painting contest," Pablo answered. "I'm the only kid, and so I paint last."

"I'll come back in an hour," Encyclopedia said bravely. His eyes hurt from watching *Sailboat in Motion* take shape. He staggered off in search of relief.

There was no relief for sore eyes anywhere in the gym. It was filled with works of modern art. The pictures appeared to have been made by throwing cans of paint into a jet engine's exhaust. The sculptures looked like pickings from a train wreck.

Encyclopedia's eyes were crossing by the time Sally rescued him.

"Come quickly," she urged. "Pablo paints next."

The boy artist was making his first brushstroke when the detectives reached the speed-painting corner.

As he worked, Pablo explained what he was painting. His landscape, *Grass in October,* took four minutes and ten seconds to complete.

Grass in October was judged good. But it was not good enough to overcome Pablo's poor time. He finished second. John Helmsly won.

"You should feel great," Sally told Pablo. "You beat all the other artists."

Pablo refused to be comforted. "Second prize is a bathroom rug," he said dejectedly. "First prize is a weekend trip to the state capital and all you can eat."

"I think John Helmsly cheated," Sally said angrily. "He used a knife."

"That isn't against the rules," Pablo muttered.

Sally wouldn't give up. "Maybe he didn't tell the truth about himself or his picture. The boat could be a whale sneezing. Encyclopedia, if you can prove John Helmsly lied, Pablo would be moved up to first place."

Encyclopedia smiled. "Of course he lied."

HOW DID ENCYCLOPEDIA KNOW?

(*Turn to page 82 for the solution to The Case of the Painting Contest.*)

The Case of Orson's Tree

Orson Merriweather had always wanted to be a tree.

"A tree is out of the rat race, settled down," he told anyone who understood such things. Orson was nine.

He used to stand around with his arms outspread, making believe he was Mr. Big of the tree world. He quit that when he was eight. A woodpecker mistook him for a dwarf oak.

Since then he put out *The Social Directory of Big Trees.* In it he listed the tallest trees of their kinds.

"If you know a tree who always wanted to

be somebody, let me know," he'd say.

Orson entered the Brown Detective Agency on Tuesday morning. He laid twenty-five cents on the gas can beside Encyclopedia.

"I'm here to hire you," he said.

"What's the problem?" Encyclopedia asked.

"My dad is bringing home a foot-high tree, a lignum vitae, this afternoon," Orson said. "I'm afraid one of the kids on the block will steal it."

"Who'd want to steal a tiny-tot tree?" Encyclopedia inquired.

"A lignum vitae is a very rare tree," Orson said. He looked embarrassed. "I've been shooting off my mouth about it to some of the kids. It can make them famous."

"Famous? Oh, that's silly," Sally protested.

"No, it isn't," Orson said. "I'm going to grow it into a national champ. Then it'll bear my name. Anyone who discovers a *biggest* tree, or grows one—*or steals one*—can name it after himself."

"A lignum vitae is one of the slowest growers on earth," Encyclopedia said. "You'll be lucky if it puts on four inches a year."

"The slower a tree grows, the more valuable it is," Orson declared.

"In a hundred years it'll be barely thirty-three feet high," Encyclopedia pointed out.

"But every inch a champ," Orson said. "My great-grandchildren will name it after me, the 'Orson Merriweather.' It'll stand in the back-yard—the tallest lignum vitae anywhere. I'll be famous!"

"What is it you want us to do?" Sally asked.

"My dad is driving up from Isle End with the tree," Orson said. "He should be home about two o'clock. Be there then and keep an eye open for tree thieves."

The detectives promised to be there. After Orson left, Sally shook her head.

"Tree thieves! What next?" she said. "Orson talks as if he just came in from the forest."

Orson lived on a block of attached, look-alike houses. Despite a light rain, the detectives arrived on time.

Nonetheless, they were too late.

"The lignum vitae has been stolen!" Orson wailed as he opened the front door. Sniffling, he told what had happened.

His father had reached home at one o'clock, an hour early. He had honked the horn, and Orson had rushed out and unloaded the tree from the trunk of the car.

"I made sure to slam the trunk lid hard because it sometimes doesn't close properly," Orson said. "I gave Dad back the trunk key, and he drove off to pick up my mom at my aunt's house."

"Why didn't your father unlock the trunk?" Encyclopedia inquired.

"He has a cold, and he didn't want to get out in the rain," Orson said. "He just opened a window and handed me the trunk key."

"Go on," Encyclopedia said.

"As I got to the front door, I heard the telephone ring," Orson continued. "The tree with all the dirt in the can weighed more than I expected. So I put it down to open the door. I ran inside to answer the phone."

"Leaving the tree outside," Encyclopedia guessed. "When you looked for it, it was gone."

"Right. The caller kept me on the line for a couple of minutes. He tried to sell me a bunch of magazines. I had a hard time telling him I was only nine."

"The telephone call was a fake to keep you inside while someone stole the tree," Sally asserted.

Encyclopedia said, "How many kids on the block did you tell that your dad was bringing the tree home today?"

"Three," Orson answered. "Ken Waite, Chuck Dugan, and Tom Winslow. The idea that you can have a tree named for you was news to them. Their mouths dropped so far, they looked like a two-car garage."

"Let's question them," Sally said eagerly.

"Good idea," Encyclopedia mumbled, while recalling the quickest way to stop a nosebleed. Tom, Ken, and Chuck were the holy terrors of the sixth grade.

Ken and Tom lived on either side of Orson. Chuck lived almost directly across the street.

Encyclopedia questioned them. It wasn't easy. Bloodshed seemed seconds away. Each boy glared at the detective's nose as if considering it as a landing spot for a punch. Then they noticed Sally standing quietly with fists clenched. They answered Encyclopedia's questions.

Chuck said, "I heard a car horn. A little later I heard a trunk lid slam. I didn't see the car. I wasn't at a window."

Tom said, "I saw Orson's father drive away

as I passed the kitchen window. I got a banana and went up to my room in the back of house. That's all I can tell you."

Ken said, "I didn't hear anything except a horn. And I sure didn't see the tree you're asking about. I was watching the ball game on television."

Back at Orson's house, Sally said glumly, "None of them said enough to mark him as the thief."

"You didn't listen," Encyclopedia said. "The thief is—"

WHO?

(*Turn to page 84 for the solution to The Case of Orson's Tree.*)

The Case of Lathrop's Hobby

When he felt up to it, Encyclopedia dropped in on Lathrop McPhee. Lathrop had the largest collection of toilet paper in Idaville.

"Millions of people collect things like dolls, stamps, and coins," Lathrop said. "I'm the only person collecting toilet paper. It's different, and it's endless. I can never have samples of all the paper in the world. The thrill is in the chase."

There wasn't room in his house to keep rolls. So Lathrop stuck with sheets. He stored them in albums in a small room off the garage.

When Encyclopedia stopped by Thursday evening, Lathrop was going over the collection with two friends, Tommy Barkdull and Paul Stanton.

"This is a big day," he said as he greeted Encyclopedia. "Wait until you see what my Uncle Arnold sent me."

He held out a hard, dimpled sheet.

"Every guest at the Hotel Calatrava in Madrid, Spain, gets a pad of these," Lathrop explained. "Uncle Arnold sent it to me for a birthday present."

"Must be nice to have someone like Uncle Arnold in the family," Encyclopedia observed.

"He sent me a newspaper clipping, too," Lathrop added. "It's about a roll of toilet paper with doodlings by a famous German artist. The roll sold for twelve thousand dollars in New York last month."

Tommy Barkdull and Paul Stanton had been leafing through Lathrop's scrapbooks. At the mention of twelve thousand dollars, both boys looked up.

"I had no idea a piece of toilet paper could ever be worth so much," Encyclopedia said.

Lathrop shrugged. "With me, it's just a

hobby. I come home and get into the collection. It's very relaxing."

Encyclopedia began looking through an album of French toilet paper. Lathrop took him by the arm.

"C'mon up to my room. I've got two new sheets that'll interest you. Tommy and Paul have already seen them."

The two sheets were English. One was from the Imperial War Museum in London. The other was from the Duke of Marlborough's castle. Each had GOVERNMENT PROPERTY printed on it.

The two boys spent half an hour in the bedroom talking toilet paper. Lathrop not only owned sheets from fifty-nine countries, but also he was a bathroom scholar.

When they returned to the storage room, Lathrop began tidying up. Suddenly he uttered a cry. "The sheet Uncle Arnold sent me from Spain! Where is it?"

The room filled with questions. Had he taken the sheet upstairs? Where had he seen it last? When?

Lathrop couldn't remember.

At Encyclopedia's suggestion, the boys

searched the house. Tommy Barkdull and Paul Stanton searched downstairs. Lathrop and Encyclopedia searched upstairs.

"We're wasting time," Lathrop grumbled. "I didn't lose the sheet. It was stolen. We ought to search Tommy and Paul. They must think the sheet is worth big bucks, but it's not."

"You can ask to search them," Encyclopedia said. "But if either Tommy or Paul is innocent, he'll be insulted. You'll lose him as a friend."

The detective paused thoughtfully.

Then he said, "The guilty boy may try to hide the sheet and return for it later. Let's wait."

To be sure that the sheet hadn't just been misplaced, Lathrop and Encyclopedia looked all over the second floor. The sheet wasn't there.

Tommy and Paul hadn't been any luckier.

"Why don't you search *us*?" Tommy suggested. "We didn't steal the sheet. Wait . . . Paul was searching in the garage a long time. He could have hidden the sheet in there."

"You've got beans up your nose if you think I'm a thief," Paul snapped. "What were you folding in the bathroom a few minutes ago?"

"I wasn't folding anything," Tommy retorted. "I was searching. Don't try to pin this on me!"

"Take it easy, both of you," Encyclopedia said. "Maybe we should look in the garage and the bathroom."

Neither Paul nor Tommy objected. The four boys went into the garage first.

Lathrop checked among the garden tools. Encyclopedia looked through a pile of wood chips and paint cans by the vise on the workbench. Paul and Tommy watched each other as they searched the shelves.

The search took fifteen minutes. The sheet of Spanish paper was nowhere to be found.

The boys went into the bathroom.

"What do you make of this?" Lathrop asked. He picked three yellow pills out of the wastebasket.

Encyclopedia opened the medicine cabinet above the sink. He took down a tiny silver pillbox.

"Here it is," he said. He pulled out the hard sheet of Spanish toilet paper. It had been folded in half eight times to make it fit into the emptied pillbox.

"What did I tell you?" Paul said triumphantly.

"You're nuts," Tommy cried. "Okay, I was in the bathroom searching while Lathrop and Encyclopedia were upstairs. But I never touched the pillbox."

Lathrop nudged Encyclopedia out of the bathroom.

"It looks like Tommy is guilty," he said. "On the other hand, maybe he's telling the truth. That means Paul is lying, which makes *him* guilty."

Lathrop shook his head sadly.

"They are both my friends," he said. "The one who is the thief is trying to blame the other. If we only had a clue."

"We have two," Encyclopedia corrected.

WHAT WERE THE CLUES?

(*Turn to page 86 for the solution to The Case of Lathrop's Hobby.*)

The Case of the Leaking Tent

When Encyclopedia and his pal Charlie Stewart went camping, they proved their courage.

They took Benny Breslin along.

Everyone liked Benny when he was standing up. It was when he lay down in bed that he made enemies.

There was no ignoring his snoring. At night his wheezes, gasps, and snorts sounded like boilers bursting up and down the block.

"Has Benny got a pair of nostrils—and a pair of lungs," Charlie Stewart said woefully. "His new tent had better work."

Benny's father had bought him a special pup tent. It was heavily lined and supposedly soundproof.

"It'll work, wait and see," Encyclopedia said.

"What has *seeing* got to do with it?" Charlie protested. "Benny can't snore anyone blind, just deaf."

The two boys were biking to Benny's house. Encyclopedia had a pup tent strapped on his back. Charlie had the fishing poles and a knapsack filled with sandwiches and juices. Their saddlebags bulged with camping gear.

Benny was waiting for them by his front door. His back and his bike were loaded for the overnight outing.

The camping grounds lay at the south end of the State Park. The boys arrived early enough to claim the best site.

Benny's new tent was blue with red piping. Encyclopedia fingered a flap. The canvas was as thick as leather.

"You can blow a trumpet in there and no one will hear you," Benny said proudly.

"So what?" Charlie whispered to Encyclopedia. "Who can blow a trumpet as loud as Benny's nose?"

Encyclopedia and Charlie pitched their tent as far from Benny's as they dared. Any farther would have been an insult. Any closer meant shock waves.

The boys were throwing a football when two sixth-graders, John Carter and Gower Bell, biked up. They looked at Benny and paled. They retreated as if they'd seen a hurricane approaching.

They put up their tent at what seemed a safe distance. Then they came over and joined in throwing the football.

After an hour everyone tired of the game. Gower Bell knew a fishing spot along the shore. The boys got their rods and headed for the ocean.

As they slid down a brambly slope, John Carter let out an "Ouch!" A thorn was stuck deep in his finger.

"I'll get it out," Gower Bell said. "Be right back."

He went to their tent and returned with a tiny sewing kit. It held three needles and some white thread. He sterilized a needle by burning the tip with a match, and dug out the thorn. For protection he spread some disinfectant jelly over the wound and bound it with a strip of adhesive bandage.

John Carter had the bandage, but Benny had the touch. No one else landed a fish. Benny caught two yellowtails, a red snapper, and a sheepshead, plus some dirty looks from John and Gower.

Encyclopedia built a fire and Benny fried the fish. After eating, the five boys sat around the fire and talked baseball and teachers till it was time to turn in.

"How soon before Benny falls asleep?" Charlie asked anxiously.

"Too soon," Encyclopedia replied.

Within five minutes Benny's soundproof tent was given its first field test. It flunked.

"Sounds like Benny is sawing wood," Encyclopedia said.

"Sounds like he's cutting down a lumberyard," Charlie corrected. "Here, have a couple."

He handed Encyclopedia two balls of cotton. The detective plugged his ears. The cotton didn't help.

An hour passed. Encyclopedia heard a raindrop, and then another and another. All at

once, rain was drumming on the tent.

Charlie moaned. "Benny finally did it. He snored up a storm!"

Hour after hour, the snores and the storm did battle.

"Benny's winning," Charlie muttered.

It was midnight before the two friends fell asleep, exhausted.

The rain had stopped when Benny woke them at dawn. "Someone ruined my new tent," he blurted.

Encyclopedia and Charlie took a look. Benny's new tent was full of tiny holes.

"Who would do such a mean thing?" Benny said. He seemed on the verge of tears.

"Didn't you hear or see anyone last night?" Charlie asked.

"I had my head in my bedroll, trying to keep dry," Benny replied. "It was like sleeping in a car wash."

Encyclopedia examined the muddy ground around Benny's tent. He found an adhesive bandage like the one Gower Bell had put on John Carter's finger. Beside the bandage was a penny.

"Did you find something?" Benny asked.

The detective picked up the muddy bandage and penny. "These."

Benny's face brightened. "Are they clues?"

Encyclopedia nodded slowly, thoughtfully. "But they only tell how the holes in the tent were made, not who made them."

"I know who made them," Charlie said. "Gower Bell and John Carter. Benny's snoring kept them awake, so they put holes in his tent, the dirty rats!"

Charlie was all for marching over to Gower Bell and John Carter and knocking heads. Encyclopedia calmed him down.

The detective had a better way.

"We can use the bandage and the penny to get them to confess," he said.

HOW?

(*Turn to page 88 for the solution to The Case of the Leaking Tent.*)

The Case of the Worm Pills

Olivia Bent put twenty-five cents on the gasoline can beside Encyclopedia.

"I need protection," she announced.

"From whom?" Encyclopedia asked, sitting up.

"From myself. I'm getting greedy again," Olivia explained. "Wilford Wiggins has a new money-making plan, and I want to believe him. He promises to make all us little kids so rich we can have a charge account with the ice-cream truck."

"Oh, no," Sally groaned. "Wilford never quits!"

Wilford Wiggins was a high-school dropout and too lazy to walk in his sleep. He spent his time dreaming up ways to cheat the children of the neighborhood out of their savings.

"Wilford has more pipe dreams than a plumber," Sally said.

"You must understand him," Encyclopedia said. "Wilford isn't well. He's suffers from ergasophobia—fear of work."

"Wilford has called a secret meeting for five o'clock in the city dump," Olivia informed the detectives. "He told us kids to bring all our money."

"Wilford didn't tell me about the meeting," Encyclopedia pointed out.

"Wilford knows he can't get anything out of you but trouble," Olivia replied. "You've stopped his phony get-rich-quick deals all summer."

"Stay home and save your money," Sally urged. "Wilford is so crooked, he once tried to sell ashes from a campfire as instant log cabins. All you had to do was add water."

"I know," Olivia admitted. "But today may be different. He may have a really good deal. I want you to listen to him and give me your opinion."

Encyclopedia looked at his watch. It was a quarter to five. "If we're going to catch him, we'd better hurry."

They reached the city dump as Wilford was about to start his sales pitch. He signaled the crowd of children to gather around him. At his feet was a large box of dirt and a sprinkling can filled with water.

Standing beside Wilford was Melvin Pugh. Melvin called himself Idaville's leading boy inventor.

"Oh, my," Sally gasped. "Double trouble."

Encyclopedia knew what she meant. Wilford and Melvin had teamed up once before, trying to peddle a bowling ball without holes. It was supposed to be for women who were afraid of breaking their fingernails.

"I'll bet the big deal today is a better mousetrap," Sally said.

"Or how to breed dumb mice," Encyclopedia replied.

Wilford had raised his hands for silence.

"You're itching to know why all the secrecy," he said. "Okay, I'll tell you. I want to keep this chance of a lifetime strictly for my young friends."

He paused. He had spotted Encyclopedia

and Sally standing with Olivia.

"This deal is so big that even smarty detectives will beg me to let them in," he said, winking at his audience.

"Quit banging your gums," someone hollered. "Get to the point."

"Can't wait to be rich, eh, friend?" Wilford shot back. "What is it that will make you oodles of money, you ask? Am I right? Well, you're looking at it!"

He pointed to the box of dirt at his feet.

"Yes, I'm talking about this box," he cried, and kicked it triumphantly. "Behold, a fortune!"

Bugs Meany pushed to the front of the crowd.

"Has anybody weighed your head lately?" Bugs demanded. "What's so great about a box of dirt?"

"I knew you'd ask, friend," Wilford said. "This box is full of worms."

"I don't see a thing," Bugs grumbled.

"You will as soon as my partner, Melvin Pugh, brings them up. Show 'em your magic pill, the greatest little outdoor invention since tent pegs."

Melvin took a white pill from his pocket. He

held it up for all to see before dropping it into the can of water. "Now watch the worms come up!" he sang, sprinkling the box of dirt.

The children crowded around, waiting for results. They waited and waited.

After what seemed hours, a worm wiggled to the surface. Then another and another. Eventually twelve worms lay upon the wet dirt.

"Did you see that?" Wilford screamed with excitement. "I put twelve worms in this box. Melvin's magic pill brought every one out into the open."

"Yucky, yucky, who cares about worms?" a girl said.

"Fishermen!" The word burst from Wilford as if he couldn't hold it back any longer. "Do you know how many fishermen there are in Idaville? Thousands! Every one of 'em needs cheap live bait—like *worms.*"

"You can start your own worm business," Melvin said, his voice as sweet as the sight of cash. "Buy a bottle of my magic worm pills and sprinkle your backyard. If you don't want to dirty your hands, sprinkle your front yard. You'll sweep the little darlings off the sidewalk like so many dollar bills."

Wilford said, "For today only, I'm offering

you a special low, low rate. A bottle of twenty of the magic worm pills for only five dollars!"

The children chattered excitedly. There was money to be had in selling worms to fishermen, all right. The pills made it easy—and gave a little kid the chance to start a business.

"What do you think, Encyclopedia? Should I buy a bottle of Melvin's pills?" Olivia asked.

"Buy his pills and all you'll get is a soaking," the detective replied.

WHAT WAS WRONG WITH THE PILLS?

(Turn to page 90 for the solution to The Case of the Worm Pills.)

Solution to
The Case of the Masked Robber

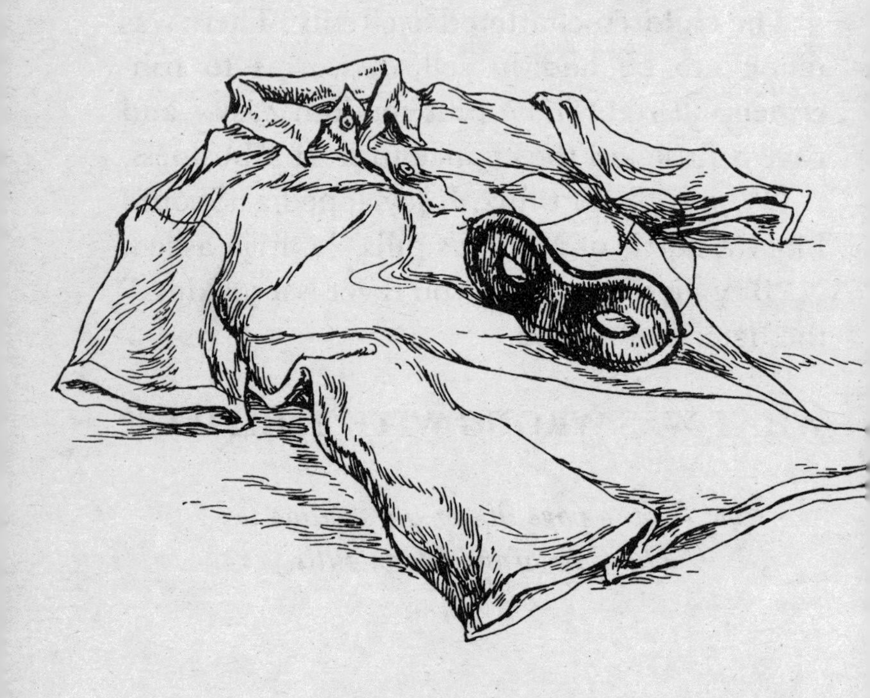

Mr. Crandan said the robber was wearing a short-sleeved shirt. So he must have seen the robber's forearms.

The racquet arm of a tennis professional like Carl Enright, who played for twenty years, would be heavily developed. Thus, if the robber had one forearm much thicker than the other, he was Carl. If both forearms were about the same size, he was Fred, the store clerk.

Mr. Crandan, himself a tennis teacher, could have immediately told whether the robber was Carl or Fred by the forearms. The fact that he didn't proved he had lied.

He had hoped to collect the insurance money, throw suspicion on one of the Enrights, and still keep the three screens.

Solution to
The Case of the Round Pizza

Bugs said, "We Tigers share everything equally. We each had a couple of pieces, so you can have the last one."

He was telling the truth—almost—and that was his mistake.

If Bugs and his two Tigers had each eaten two pieces, there would not have been an odd number, such as one, left in the box.

Pizzas are sliced into an even number of

pieces. The Tigers ate six. Thus there would have been an even number of pieces left in the box if Bugs had come with a whole pie.

So Bugs had brought to the clubhouse an odd number of pieces. One piece was missing—the piece he stole from Farnsworth before he took the whole pizza.

Trapped by Encyclopedia's sharp brain, Bugs took up a collection and bought Farnsworth another pizza.

Solution to
The Case of Bugs's Zebra

Bugs had one of his Tigers call Sally, say he was Phil Birch, and hire her to pick up the shopping bag at the zoo.

Bugs had to have a reason for being at the zoo when the detectives arrived. He had to be able to say he saw them feeding the antelopes sweets.

So he said he was sketching a zebra.

Actually, he had drawn the zebra at home

from memory. That was his mistake!

Had he drawn the zebra from sight, he would not have had one of the body stripes "running from the front to the hind legs."

Body stripes on a zebra do not run side to side, but up and down.

Bugs confessed, snarled, and slunk out of the zoo.

Solution to
The Case of the Treasure Hunt

Having spied on Mr. McPherson, Regina knew the last clue was: "Look beneath the best-known dairy in town." She also knew the "You Won" card was under the windshield wiper of the pickup truck there.

So Encyclopedia told Mr. McPherson "to switch two letters," the *a* and the *i* in *dairy*. Now the last clue read: "Look beneath the best-known diary in town."

During the treasure hunt Regina merely glanced at it. She missed the change in spelling and gave herself away. She went to the original site, under the dairy office building.

Thanks to Encyclopedia, the "You Won" card was moved to the main library, where the treasure hunt had started.

The card was taped under the glass display case that housed Samuel Dowdy's diary.

Solution to
The Case of the Stolen Jewels

Dustin overheard the tall man tell the short man not to write down the exact address of the house on Highland Avenue but to keep it in his head.

To help the short man's memory, the tall man said, "Just remember—it's the last upside-down year. The next one won't come for more than four thousand years."

So Encyclopedia knew the number of the

house on Highland Avenue was 1961.

That was "the last upside-down year," and "the next one" (which "won't come for more than four thousand years") will be 6009.

Upside down, the years 1961 and 6009 read the same as right-side up!

Solution to
The Case of the Painting Contest

John Helmsly claimed that he was a sea captain. He believed that a picture of a boat painted by a sea captain would favorably influence the judges.

However, he used words no sea captain would use.

He said, "The boat is moving at about only four knots an hour." A "knot" means a nautical mile per hour. So what he actually said was, "The boat is moving at about only four knots an hour an hour." Nonsense!

He also said "front" instead of "bow," "back" instead of "stern," and "map" instead of "chart."

When Encyclopedia pointed out his mistakes to the judges, John Helmsly confessed. He was really a professional artist.

He withdrew from the contest, and first prize was awarded to Pablo.

Solution to The Case of Orson's Tree

Ken was innocent, But Chuck and Tom stole the tree. Chuck's mistake gave them away.

Chuck said he heard "a trunk lid slam." But he also said he "didn't see the car."

Unless he had seen Orson remove the tree from the car's trunk, he could not have known it was a trunk lid that slammed. He would have assumed it was a car door that slammed!

When Encyclopedia pointed out his error, Chuck confessed. From his house across the street, he had watched for the tree to be delivered.

When he saw Orson carrying the tree to the door, he alerted Tom. Then he phoned Orson's house. He kept Orson talking while Tom stole the tree.

Chuck and Tom returned the tree.

Solution to
The Case of Lathrop's Hobby

The first clue was the hard sheet of paper, which had been "folded in half eight times" in order to fit it into the tiny pillbox.

The second clue was the vise in the garage.

Paul couldn't fold the paper small enough by hand, so he used the vise. Then he tried to make Encyclopedia and Lathrop believe he had seen Tommy folding something in the bathroom.

He was so eager to blame Tommy that he didn't think. Using only his hands, Tommy couldn't have folded the paper eight times, either.

Encyclopedia knew this. No one can fold anything more than seven times by hand.

Solution to
The Case of the Leaking Tent

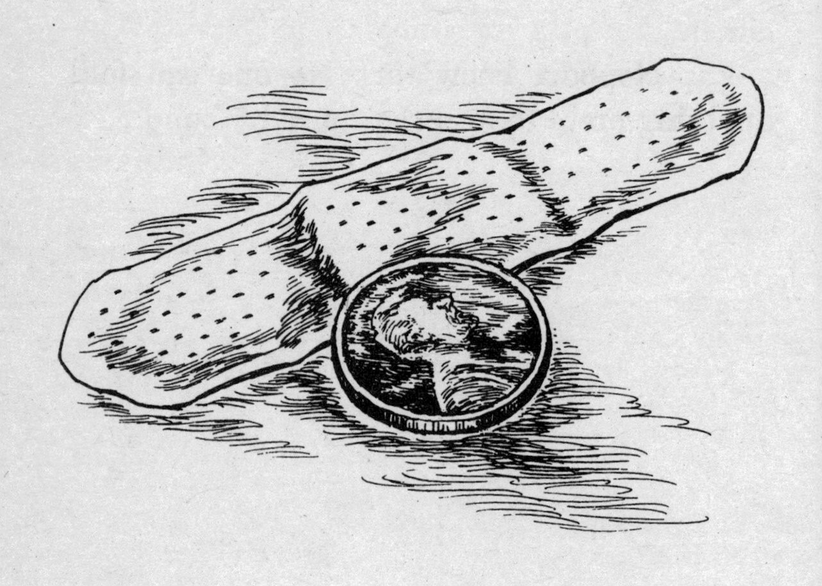

Jealous of Benny's fishing prowess, and kept awake by his snoring, Gower and John sought revenge. They put holes in his tent with a needle. At first they failed. The tent was "thick as leather."

So Gower (it turned out) used a bandage to tape a penny to his forefinger. He used the penny as a thimble to push the needle through the canvas.

After making many holes, he dropped the needle. He took the bandage off in order to pick it up. The bandage and the penny were left in the mud, meaningless to anyone who might find them. Or so Gower and John thought.

They had not counted on Encyclopedia's sharp brain.

The detective scared them. He made them believe that the penny held a fingerprint.

Gower confessed, and his father bought Benny a new tent.

Solution to The Case of the Worm Pills

Encyclopedia realized the pill wasn't responsible for bringing the worms up from the dirt. The water alone was.

Worms dwell in underground tunnels that flood when it rains. They work their way to the surface in order to breathe.

That's exactly what they did when Melvin poured water (with the fake pill dissolved in it) on the box of dirt.

Encyclopedia explained this to the children. No one bought a bottle of the pills. Wilford and Melvin were left without a sale.

Wilford walked over to Encyclopedia and admitted that the pill was just sugar.

Then he grumbled, "Why don't you go somewhere and get stupid!"

About the Author

DONALD J. SOBOL is the award-winning author of more than sixty-five books for young readers. He lives in Florida with his wife, Rose, who is also an author. They have three grown children. The Encyclopedia Brown books have been translated into fourteen languages.